Thomas

ALL FOR A DIME!

A Bear and Mole Story

Will Hillenbrand

Holiday House / New York

To Sawako, I love drawing with you. . . . You inspire me.

HOLIDAY HOUSE is registered in the U.S. Patent and Trademark Office.
Printed and Bound in April 2015 at Toppan Leefung, DongGuan City, China.
The artwork was created with 6B graphite pencil, colored pencil, chalk pastel, pixels, china marker,
crayon, ink, watercolor, collage, transparent tape and kneaded eraser on paper/canvas.
www.holidayhouse.com
First Edition

Library of Congress Cataloging-in-Publication Data
Hillenbrand, Will, author, illustrator.
All for a dime! : a Bear and Mole story / Will Hillenbrand. — First edition.
pages cm
Summary: Bear has no trouble selling his berries at the farmers' market, but Mole and Skunk are less successful
with their worms and perfume.
ISBN 978-0-8234-2946-2 (hardcover)
[1. Farmers' markets—Fiction. 2. Bears—Fiction. 3. Moles (Animals)—Fiction. 4. Skunks—Fiction.] I. Title.
PZ7.H55773Al 2015
[E]—dc23
2013038990

Mole pushed aside some dirt.
He picked up worms.
Yum. Yum. Yum.
He put some into his pail.

Bear pushed aside leaves.
He picked berries.
Yum. Yum. Yum.
He filled up his pail.

"Skunk loves berries.
I'll pick some just for her."

Knock. Knock. Knock.

"Fresh berries just for you!"

"Thank you!" Skunk grinned.
"I love blueberries!"
"Look what else I have, worms!"
Mole beamed.
"N-n-nice," stuttered Skunk.

"Look what I made, perfume."
Skunk smiled.

Puff. Puff. Puff.

"N-n-nice," stuttered Bear.
"Now we all have something to sell
on Market Day," said Mole.
"We should make lots of money."
Skunk winked.
"Lots," agreed Mole.

On Market Day Bear, Mole
and Skunk made signs.

They collected stools.

They packed.

They put up tents

and set out the goods.

Bear was busy.

Mole and Skunk waited and waited and waited.

"Nothing is selling. Let's switch seats to change our luck," suggested Mole.

"That's better."
Skunk grinned.
"I would like
to buy some of your
lovely perfume."
"That will be a dime."
Mole smiled.

Puff.
Puff. Puff.

"Now I would like to buy some of those scrumptious worms," said Mole.
"That will be a dime."
Skunk smiled.

"A little more perfume, please," said Skunk.
"Gladly, that will be a dime." Mole chuckled.

slurp.
slurp.
slurp.

"I would be happy to claim the rest of those worms," said Mole.
"That will be a dime," said Skunk.

Puff!
Puff!
Puff!

Mole yawned. "What a busy day, I'm exhausted."
Skunk yawned. "Me too, but we sold out!"
"I bet we made lots of money.
Let's count it up!" said Mole.

CHA-CHING!

"I have a dime!"
Skunk beamed.
"I don't have anything,"
mumbled Mole.

"Hummmmm," fretted Skunk.
"We don't have anything left but a dime,
yet we were busy all day."
"We had fun too.
That's good,"
mused Mole.

"That is enough for another Market Day!" said Bear.

"Sell anything?"
asked Mole.

"All but these," said Bear.
"And we can put those on top of the ice cream
I bought with my dimes!"